This book belongs to:

Kathryn

A catalogue record for this book is available from the British Library

Published by Ladybird Books Ltd
A Penguin Company
Penguin Books Ltd, 80 Strand, London WC2R 0RL, UK
Penguin Books Australia Ltd, Camberwell, Victoria, Australia
Penguin Group (NZ) Ltd, 67 Apollo Drive, Rosedale, North Shore 0632, New Zealand

15
© LADYBIRD BOOKS LTD MCMXCVIII. This edition MMVI

ISBN-13: 978-1-84646-068-5

Printed in China

Little
Red Hen

illustrated by Graham Percy

The wheat

The dog

The cat

The flour

4

Little Red Hen

The rat

The bread

"Will you help me
plant the wheat?"
asked Little Red Hen.

"No," said the rat,
the cat and the dog.

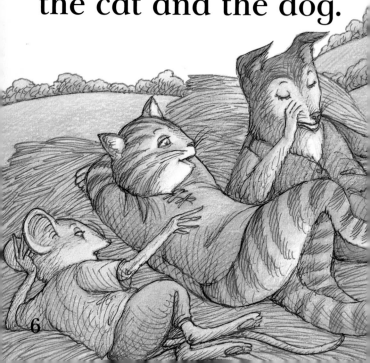

6

"Then I will plant it all by myself," said Little Red Hen.

And she did.

"Will you help me
cut the wheat?"
asked Little Red Hen.

"No," said the rat,
the cat and the dog.

11

"Then I will cut it all by myself," said Little Red Hen.

And she did.

"Will you help me make the flour?" asked Little Red Hen.

"No," said the rat, the cat and the dog.

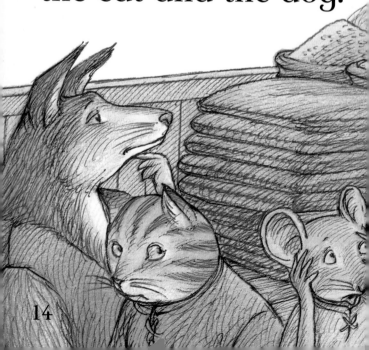

"Then I will make it all by myself," said Little Red Hen.

And she did.

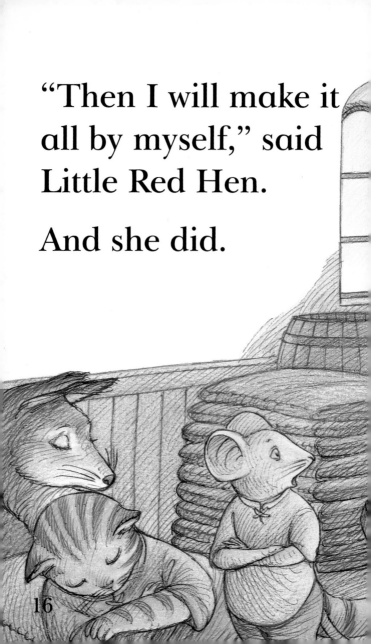

"Will you help me make the bread?" asked Little Red Hen.

"No," said the rat, the cat and the dog.

"Then I will make it
all by myself," said
Little Red Hen.

And she did.

"Will you help me
eat the bread?"
asked Little Red Hen.

"Yes," said the rat,
the cat and the dog.

© 1993 Geddes & Grosset Ltd
Reprinted 1994
Published by Geddes & Grosset Ltd,
New Lanark, Scotland.

ISBN 1 85534 576 5

Printed and bound in Slovenia.

Puss in Boots

Retold by Judy Hamilton
Illustrated by Lindsay Duff

Tarantula Books

There was once a young man who moved from place to place doing odd jobs for a living. His constant companion was a cat with no name.

Lately, the man had found little work, and had grown poorer and poorer. Now he had only a few coins left.

"I am afraid I shall have to give you away, puss," he said sadly.

"I haven't enough money left to feed you."

To his surprise the cat spoke back to him.

"Use the money you have to buy me a pair of boots," said the cat, "and I shall make us both rich."

His master was so surprised to hear the cat speak that he went to the cobbler's straight away, and bought a beautiful pair of boots with the last of his money.

The cat put the boots on, picked up his master's sack, and vanished.

Still amazed by his talking pet, the man sat down on a tree stump and waited.

After a long time the cat returned with a rabbit in the sack.

"See what I caught for our supper!" he said proudly.

"That's all very well, puss," replied his master, "but I thought you were going to make us rich! All this time, and only one rabbit!"

"Not just one rabbit," said the cat. "Lots of rabbits I took all the other rabbits that I caught to the palace, and asked to see His Majesty the King. What a fine and noble man he is! I bowed very low and then handed over my bag of rabbits. 'Your Majesty,' I said to him, 'please accept these rabbits with the humble good wishes of my master and myself. They will make a tasty supper for you and your courtiers'."

The cat's master did not really believe this story, but was glad to have some food to eat, so he cooked the rabbit for supper and said nothing.

Cat and master slept soundly that night, and then very early the next morning, the cat hurried off mysteriously once more. A while later, he reappeared in a great state of excitement.

"Hurry up, master!" he cried, "Take off all your clothes, and jump into the river!"

"You must be joking!" protested the young man.

"Please, master, trust me!" implored puss. "Just do what I ask and soon you will be a wealthy man!"

"Oh well, it is rather hot today. I suppose a swim would be nice and refreshing," sighed the young man. He slipped off his clothes and jumped into the river with a splash.

Puss picked up all his master's clothes and hurriedly stuffed them down a rabbit hole nearby.

"Now, the King!" he muttered, and ran off, leaving his poor naked master stranded in midstream.

The young man splashed about aimlessly, becoming more and more worried as time passed.

Suddenly a magnificent carriage came into view. It had a golden crown on each door, and the young man guessed it was the royal coach.

Imagine his surprise when the carriage stopped by the riverbank and the cat, boot buckles twinkling in the sun, sprang out followed by the king and his daughter!

Embarrassed, the young man tried to hide under the water.

"Your majesty," he said respectfully. "that is my master, the Duke of Carabas, having his daily swim."

"Tell your master that I should like to meet him in person," commanded the king. "I must thank him for the gifts which you brought."

The cat scuttled over to his master.

"What's going on, puss?" asked the young man.

"Shh .... Stay there and say nothing! This won't take long!" urged the cat.

Returning to where the king stood, the cat bowed.

"Your majesty, my master is in no state to meet you. Some thieves have run off with all his clothes!"

"Poor fellow!" exclaimed the king, and turning to one of his servants he said, "run to the palace and find some decent clothes for this young man!"

The young man was soon dressed in clothes of the finest material—as noble as a duke.

"Come and dine with me tonight," said the king. "Your clever cat has given my cook a wonderful recipe for cooking the rabbits which you sent."

The cat smiled secretly. His plan was working!

The young man was amazed, but accepted the king's invitation graciously.

"I shall return you safely home in my carriage after dinner," said the king.

"And I shall be back in time to lead the way to my master's palace," announced the cat, and bowing low, he ran off.

His master was puzzled. "Palace? What Palace?" he thought.

The cat sped on in his smart boots, swift as the wind, until he came to an enormous castle which he knew belonged to a fearsome giant. Unafraid, he scratched at the door.

The giant answered the door, towering above the cat.

"What do you want?" he bellowed.

"If I can sleep by your fire, I will catch all the mice in this castle," announced the cat.

"I have no mice here. Go away!" roared the giant and was just about to slam the door shut when the cat slipped between his legs and into the castle. Quick as a flash he scuttled across the grand hallway and into the enormous drawingroom where a large fire burned merrily in the grate.

The giant thundered in after the cat.

"Just what do you think you are doing?" he demanded.

The cat paid no attention to this. Instead, he simply asked, "Can you work magic?"

"Magic? I'll show you magic you cheeky animal I can change myself into a lion! That will scare you off!" said the giant triumphantly.

But the cat did not look in the least bit scared. H just smiled.

"I expect it's quite easy for a giant to change himself into something big and fierce, like a lion," said the cat. "But I don't expect you are clever enough to turn yourself into something really small and timid, like a mouse, for example!"

The giant was furious at this suggestion.

"Me? Not clever enough?" he spluttered with indignation. "I'll show you! Just watch this!" Whoosh! Within an instant the giant was gone. In his place, right in front of the cat's nose, was a tiny brown mouse.

The cat pounced, and swallowed up the mouse in one great gulp. The giant was gone!

While all this had been going on, the cat's young master had been dining with the king and his daughter the princess. The meal had been splendid, and the young man had had a lovely time talking with the beautiful princess and her father.

They had just finished eating when the cat returned.

"Your Majesty, allow me to direct your carriage to my master's palace," said the cat.

And so they all set off in the royal coach.

The cat directed the way to the giant's castle.

"This is the home of my master the Duke of Carabas," announced the cat.

The young man was amazed, but said nothing and allowed the cat to lead the royal party inside the palace.

The king was very impressed. "You must be a young man of great importance," he said. "And I have come to like and respect you a great deal in the short time that I have known you. My daughter too has become fond of you."

This of course, was the beginning of another story, for in a very short time the young man and the princess were married and had a long and happy life together.

Puss lived a comfortable life at the palace, dozing by the great fire with his boots by his side.

His master thought he was the cleverest cat in the world, and he probably was.

Good old Puss in Boots!